The Kite Festival

LEYLA TORRES

Farrar Straus Giroux · New York

To Alejandra, Eliana, and Andrés

Copyright © 2004 by Leyla Torres

All rights reserved

Distributed in Canada by Douglas & McIntyre Ltd.

Color separations by Hong Kong Scanner Arts

Printed and bound in the United States of America by Berryville Graphics

Designed by Nancy Goldenberg

First edition, 2004

10 9 8 7 6 5 4 3 2 1

Library of Congress Cataloging-in-Publication Data

Torres, Leyla.

    The kite festival / Leyla Torres.— 1st ed.

      p. cm.

    Summary: While on a Sunday outing, Fernando and his family encounter a kite festival and decide to create a kite from scrap materials so that they can join in.

    ISBN 0-374-38054-6

    [1. Kites—Fiction.   2. Family life—Fiction.   3. Hispanic Americans—Fiction.]   I. Title.

PZ7.T6457Ki 2004

[E]—dc21

                           2003044060

Early one Sunday morning, Fernando and his grandfather were studying the map at their kitchen table.

"Where should we go on our drive today?" Fernando asked.

"Let's have a real adventure!" Grandpa Félix said. "Close your eyes and pick a spot."

Fernando shut his eyes and put his finger on the map. He and his grandfather leaned over to see what he had chosen.

"San Vicente!" Fernando said. "We've never been there before."

Mama packed a picnic lunch of roast chicken, corn cakes, tangerines, and lemonade, together with plates, cups, and paper napkins. Grandma Felisa made her delicious salsa picante and placed it in the picnic basket. She also took her knitting project, a pair of gloves that were almost finished. Papa put the map in the car and checked to make sure there was enough gas. Fernando gathered up his paper and crayons so that he could draw on the trip, and his younger sister, Flora, brought her pull-toy bear.

The Flórez family wound their way down a steep mountain road, and the air became warmer and more fragrant. Instead of the eucalyptus and cypress trees of the higher regions, banana plants and guava and orange trees dotted the landscape.

"There is San Vicente!" announced Papa as he rounded a curve. In the distance, orange tile rooftops glinted in the morning sun.

"Look, Grandpa! Look at all those kites!" Fernando cried.

In the town square, children and grownups were getting ready for a kite festival.
Fernando never imagined there could be so many different kinds of kites.

"It's too bad we didn't bring a kite," said Fernando's mother.

"I'll bet we can find one," Grandpa Félix replied with a mischievous smile.

"Look! There's a stand on the other side of the plaza," said Fernando.

Fernando and his grandfather walked over to the vendor.

"Do you sell kites?" Grandpa Félix asked.

"All I have is bamboo strips in case someone's kite frame breaks. Too bad the stores are closed today."

"We'd like three of the strips," Grandpa Félix said.

"What are you going to do with them?" Fernando asked.

"Just wait a minute and you'll see," Grandpa Félix said.

"Florencia, can we use that string attached to Flora's toy?" Grandpa Félix asked.

"Of course," said Mama as she untied it.

The Flórez family sat on the steps of the church and watched Grandpa Félix. First he cut small notches at the ends of each bamboo strip. Then he joined the strips together at their centers with a short piece of string. Another piece of string was tucked into the notches at the bamboo ends and pulled tight.

Grandpa Félix scratched his head. "Here is the frame, but now we need to find a piece of paper big enough to make the sail."

Mama rummaged around in her purse. "What if we unfold the map? Would that be big enough?"

"Sure!" Fernando shouted. "And we can decorate it with my crayons."

Grandpa Félix laid the map on the ground and cut it to size, leaving a little extra at the edge to fold over the frame. With Grandma Felisa's help, Fernando drew a big hand on the paper and filled it with color.

"How are we going to attach the paper to the frame?" Fernando asked.

Grandpa Félix looked at Papa. "Francisco, do you have any tape or glue in your toolbox?"

Papa went to the car and looked in his toolbox. He even searched under the seats and in the glove compartment.

"Look, everyone, I found some string, but no tape or glue."

For a few moments everyone was quiet. Then Fernando said, "I know what we could use! Band-Aids from the first-aid kit!"

He raced to get them from the car.

"We have to hurry, Grandpa," Fernando said as he helped his grandfather tape the sail in place.

Next Grandpa tied two pieces of string to the frame in order to make a bridle. No sooner had he finished tying the line to the bridle than a voice boomed through the loudspeaker, "Ladies and gentlemen! Welcome to the Second Annual San Vicente Kite Festival! Is everyone ready? Launch your kites to the clouds!"

"That's it," Grandpa Félix said. "Let's hope it works."

Standing close to his grandfather, Fernando gripped the line. Mama faced them, holding the kite high. A big gust of wind blew through the plaza, and Grandpa Félix gave the signal. Mama let go of the kite, and it rushed up, swooping and diving around in circles. But then it fell back to the ground.

"Your kite is missing a tail," offered a man walking by. "Without its tail, it can't settle into the breeze."

"Of course, he's right," said Grandpa Félix.

"Where will we get a tail?" Fernando asked.

"Let's make a bow tail with some of our paper napkins." In no time at all, Grandpa Félix had fashioned a tail from some napkins they found in their picnic basket.

With its long tail securely in place, the kite now quickly pulled upward.

"Ow! Ouch!" Fernando let go of the string, and the kite came back to the ground. "That hurt. The string burned my hand," he said.

"Oh, my goodness, that won't do," Grandpa Félix said. "I wonder how we could protect your hands."

"Here, put these on," said Grandma Felisa, offering Fernando the gloves she was knitting. "The left one is missing its little finger, but they're good enough to protect your hands."

When the wind picked up, Mama released the kite again, and it now climbed steadily skyward.

Abruptly, the wind changed direction, and the kite sailed toward a tall tree. Fernando and his grandfather pulled in the opposite direction, but they lost control and the kite's tail was snagged by one of the highest branches.

Fernando stamped his foot in frustration. "Oh no! We've lost our kite!"

Cautiously, Papa climbed up through the branches, but not far enough to be able to untangle the tail. Holding the kite in one hand, he tugged gently. But the paper bows were hopelessly tangled, and the tail ripped in half.

"We'll just have to make another tail," Mama said.

"Yes, but with what?" Grandpa Félix replied.

"How about your fabric belt?" Grandma Felisa asked, pointing to Mama's skirt.

"I don't know if I like that idea," replied Mama, glancing up at the tree. "I don't want to lose this belt—it's my favorite one."

"Don't worry, Florencia," said Grandpa. "We won't lose it, and besides, if you don't risk an egg, you can't get a chicken."

With its new belt tail, the kite lifted onto a steady easterly breeze.
Suddenly Fernando's line crossed the line of another kite being flown nearby.
"Don't pull your string, Fernando," warned Grandpa. "It could break."

For an instant Fernando's kite swayed and hesitated, poised to take another dive. Thinking quickly, he moved toward the other flier, and she ducked under his line. Disaster had been avoided, and both of them were relieved.

Fernando's kite gained altitude once again. Finding a strong updraft, it settled into the breeze. The family fixed their eyes on that miniature hand waving lazily from the clouds. Mama served a bite to eat while each took a turn holding the line. The Flórez family lost track of time.

The sun sat low on the horizon when Fernando began to reel in his kite. As it slowly descended, the kite and the young boy played together, back and forth, until it flickered just over his head. Behind him, Fernando's family quietly gathered up the slack line. With a final gentle tug, the kite floated softly to the ground.

The mayor of San Vicente gave out a prize for the kite that was the most beautiful and one for the kite that flew the highest. Then he announced that the Flórez family's kite was the most original. They all went to the podium, and Fernando held the kite up for all to see. Everyone cheered. The mayor shook hands with the whole family and handed them a basket of oranges.

On their return trip home, the Flórez family traveled up the mountain in their station wagon.

"Grandpa Félix, how did you learn so much about kites?" asked Fernando.

"When I was young, I made a lot of kites. I made them with my father, and we sold them every Monday at the market."

"Can we come back to the kite festival next year?"

Grandpa Félix smiled at his grandson. "Of course, my boy. We can return every year."

Making a Hexagonal Kite

With the help of an adult, it is easy to build a hexagonal—six-sided—kite.

Materials Needed 3 strips of wood, either cypress or bamboo, 28 inches long, 1/2 inch wide, and 3/16 inch thick, with a notch cut into each end · At least 125 feet of string · A piece of plastic film, 32 inches square (from a plastic trash bag) · Vinyl package tape · 1 to 5 strips of plastic film, 2 inches wide and 8 feet long

Constructing the Frame

1. Cut an 8-inch length of string and tie the 3 notched strips together at their centers. Position these strips to form a perfect hexagon (intersecting at 60-degree angles).

60 °

2. Cut an 8-foot length of string. Tie one end to the notched end of one of the strips. Tuck and loop the string into the notch of each strip as you move around the frame. The string should be tight enough to hold the strips in place at the 60-degree angle, but not enough to bend the frame.

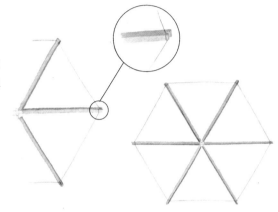

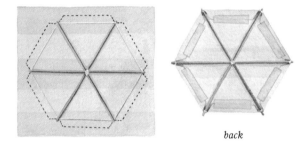

back

3. Spread the 32-inch-square plastic film out on a flat surface. Position the frame on top of the plastic. Directly on the plastic, draw a hexagonal shape 2 inches larger than the outside of the frame. Remove the frame and cut out the hexagon you have just drawn. Then cut a small triangle into each corner that will allow the frame ends to stick out, as shown in the illustration. To secure the sail to the frame, fold the 2-inch border over the frame and string and tape it down, using vinyl package tape.

Making and Attaching the Bridle to the Frame

front

4. To form the bridle, cut a 32-inch length of string. Tie one end to the end of a frame strip, and the other end to the end of an adjacent frame strip. Then cut an 18-inch length of string. Tie one end to the center of the frame. Cut a tiny hole in the center of the sail. Poke the other end through the sail to the front side of the kite and pull the string through. Loop the 32-inch length of string from the back to the front of the kite, and tie the unsecured end of the 18-inch-long string to its center.

Setting the Tail

5. Cut a 20-inch length of string. Tie each end of the string to the ends of the two adjacent strips opposite to the ends where you attached the bridle. Next tie the tail (1 to 5 strips of polyethylene film, each 8 feet long) to the center of this string.

6. Tie one end of your flying line (the remaining string) to the bridle. Take the kite to a breezy, open place and *let it fly!*

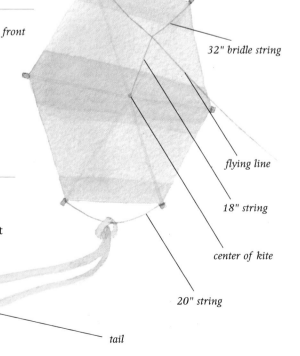

32" bridle string

flying line

18" string

center of kite

20" string

tail